D0038868

Charlie
& the Rodent Queen

by

C.A. GOODY

illustrated by

TERRY LAAKER

*To Carol -
Love & blessings,
CA Goody*

Cover design by Reid Johns and Kim Hurley
Written and Printed in the U.S.A.
Typeset by TKPrinting
Printed by Central Plains Book, a division of Sun Graphics LLC
Copyright (c) 2003 by C.A. Goody

First Printing May 2003
ISBN 978-0-9702546-2-7

Goody, C.A. 1962-
Charlie's Great Adventures
Charlie Moves to Arizona
Charlie and the Rodent Queen

Summary - Charlie the cat's life is turned upside down when his family adopts a hamster.
1 - Animal Adventure   2 - Cats   3 - Humor   4 - Children

DEDICATIONS

To My Lord Jesus Christ,
who makes all things possible.

And to Mom and Dad; who told me
I could do anything, and
supported me in everything.

Chapter 1

Charlie

H<small>I THERE; IT'S ME,</small> C<small>HARLIE</small>! You know, someone told me recently that Abyssinian cats (of which I am one) are directly related to lions. I think that sounds really cool, but I'm not sure it's true. I saw a lion once on TV, and I got the feeling he would have eaten me in one gulp before bothering to ask how distant a cousin I was. And no one in my family has table manners like that.

Anyway, as you may know, I live with my human family in a nice house. It's a great life for a cat. There's plenty of good food (even occasional table scraps if they leave the dog outside), lots of clean water (cool, fresh out of the bathtub), comfy furniture to lie on, and all the petting a cat could want. My girl Amanda goes to school, but when she comes home, we snuggle up on her bed, and she tells me about her day. She tells Mom all the things that happened in class, but she saves all the good stuff to discuss with me. You know, what happened on the playground, who has a crush on whom, which boys are cute and which ones deserve to LIVE in detention, which girls are nice and which are total snobs . . . you know, the important stuff. Every time she stops talking for a moment, I meow to let her know that I'm listening, and it seems to encourage her to keep going. I don't know who most of the people she talks about are, but I could tell you some really interesting things about every kid in her grade at school.

While Amanda is at school, I like to hang out with Andrew. He's two and always lots of fun. He's good at finding the most interesting stuff that Mom has hidden around the house. Like the other day. I was sitting under the kitchen table waiting for Mom to come in and make lunch. She was cleaning somewhere in the back of the house. Andrew toddled into the kitchen and began opening cabinet doors. I think he was supposed to be taking a nap, but since Mom was busy, he had decided to see what kind of mischief he could get into.

He pulled a few things out of each cabinet

as he went along. Nothing seemed to catch his interest for more than a minute, and nothing he pulled out was worth my time to get up off the floor, where I was resting, to go and check out. Until he opened up the corner cabinet. A big smile crossed his face when he opened the door, but I couldn't see inside to tell what he was getting excited about. Then he started pulling out Tupperware.

How, you may ask, does a cat know about Tupperware? Easy. That's the stuff Mom puts all the leftovers in. Leftovers are wonderful things. You see, Mom puts the stuff that didn't get eaten at lunch or dinner or whenever into these plastic containers called Tupperware. Then she sticks them in the refrigerator, leaves them for around three or four days, takes them back out, and asks if anyone wants them. When everyone says "no," she gives the food to me. If I don't like it, or don't eat all of it, she gives it to the dog, Frisky. I don't know why she has to age it for those few days, but as long as I get it eventually, it's okay with me.

Well, when Andrew started pulling out all the Tupperware, I got very excited. Maybe there was food in one of those things! I ran over and started sniffing each one as he pulled it out. But there was no food. Just tons and tons of containers. When the stack in front of Andrew started getting too big, he began pushing the pile farther away from him and throwing the lids across the room. They kind of looked like Frisbees, but I'm not a dog, so I refused to chase them. Even if I was tempted.

Andrew started trying to make the pile of containers in front of him into some kind of building; at least I think that was what he was doing, because he kept stacking them higher and higher. As he continued to throw and stack, I saw that there was more space inside the cabinet where he had taken things out, so I crawled in there to look around. It was huge inside, like some giant cave! It was an 'L' shaped cabinet, and when I walked around the corner, it was really dark. I could make out some more plastic things stacked up high, but they were dusty from being shoved away where no one could reach them.

Suddenly, in the back corner where it was the darkest, something moved. Something very small and quick. It was a bug! You remember how much I like to chase bugs, right? Well, this was really exciting, because it was dark, and we were in cramped quarters, and I was on his territory, so this bug had the advantage. Could I get him? And if I did, would he be tasty?

I had to wait patiently and quietly to make my move. This wasn't easy with Andrew crashing around in the cabinet behind me, but I stayed perfectly still, in pounce position, waiting. Finally, that little bug crept forward about two inches, and I felt I could get him without smashing my nose in the corner. I pounced.

Well, I would have gotten him. If only my right elbow hadn't bumped into that stack of containers halfway through my attack. Since it did, the plastic bowls fell on top of me. First I screeched out a "meow," and then I started sneezing like crazy. You see, the dust went flying all over the place, and as the bowls continued to roll forward around the corner and to the front of the cabinet, the dust spread.

Andrew let out a kind of yelp as he saw the bowls rolling toward him. I guess he thought the Tupperware was fighting back and trying to attack him for throwing its friends around. Whatever the reason, he let out that little scream, and then he started sneezing. I made my way out of the cabinet and sat next to him on the floor.

That's how Mom found us. She came running into the room and saw us sitting side by side on the kitchen floor surrounded by huge stacks of containers and sneezing our heads off. The floor was totally covered in plastic, from one end of the room to the other. She didn't look happy.

Andrew looked up at her and saw the angry expression beginning to form on her face. "Chawlic did it," he said.

What, me? I'm just sitting here, minding my own business, sneezing. That's what I tried to say to Mom with my eyes, as I looked up at her. I couldn't believe my buddy Andrew was blaming it all on me.

"Charlie did this all by himself, did he?" Mom asked.

"Uh huh," Andrew said solemnly.

That's when I saw it. Andrew didn't notice, because he had his head down trying to look like an innocent little angel. But I saw it. Mom was working very hard to look mad, but I could see that she was trying not to laugh. She was looking at me, looking at the mess, and trying to figure out if Andrew thought she would really buy the idea that I created this disaster area all by myself. And it was cracking her up, but she didn't want us to know.

"My, he's been a very busy cat. Are you sure you didn't help him out just a little?" she asked. "That's an awfully high tower for Charlie to build."

"Um, well, he musta stood up on his back paws," Andrew stated.

"Charlie, I'm so impressed. That is an amazing building," Mom came over and started petting me.

I looked at Andrew. "Meow," I said, trying to get his attention. Mom was baiting him. I could tell. And even though he had tried to throw me to the wolves by blaming the whole mess on me, I still felt I should warn him. "Meow," I said again.

He wasn't paying attention to me. He was looking at his building, and listening to Mom. "I must say, that really is an incredible building. Look at the designs he made with the different colors. That is one intelligent cat," Mom went on.

"Well, I hepped him a wittle," Andrew said.

"Still, Charlie must have done most of it for you to give him the credit," Mom said, petting me even more.

"Meow!" I was still trying to warn him.

But he wasn't listening. He'd had all he could stand of someone else getting credit for his work. "I did it! I did it all. All Chawlie did was knock some bowls ova' and make it dusty," he added, looking very proud of himself.

"Oh, well then, you can clean up all this mess young man," the angry tone was back in Mom's voice, "and I'll sweep up the dust Charlie spread around when you're done."

"Ah, mom," Andrew whined, looking around the room. "It wiw take me fowevew to cwean all dis up."

"If you don't like cleaning up messes, don't make them," Mom said. Then she looked at me and shook her head. "Now all I have to do is teach you how to use a broom."

But she was just kidding. I had a great life here, no one ever treated me badly, and I never got into too much trouble. I was the King of the House, the Prince of my Realm, the Ruler of my Domain.

At least I was. Until someone came in and declared herself queen.

It was a busy week. Grandma from Denver was staying at the house for a few days. Only she wasn't really from Denver (wherever that is). She was actually from someplace called Germany, and she spoke with the cutest accent. She almost sounded like Andrew sometimes, saying the right words but not quite the same way everyone else did or having to stop and think for a couple of moments to come up with the correct word. I loved to listen to her. Sometimes, when she was very excited about something, in the middle of a sentence, she would switch over to this other language. I couldn't understand a word she said, but it sounded really neat and exotic. Dad could understand a lot of what she said when she spoke that way, but I think he understood the emotion, not the actual words.

Anyway, Omi (that's what the kids called her; it means Grandma in German) was getting ready to go back home. It had really been fun having her around, but she said she had to get back to her house and her friends.

"Before I go," she said to Amanda and Andrew in her cool accent, "I want to buy you a present."

"YES!" Amanda yelled.

"YEAH!" Andrew shouted.

"What would you like?" Omi asked with a big smile on her face. "Not too much money, because I'm not a rich one, okay?"

Amanda and Andrew started whispering to each other. I was straining trying to hear them, but Omi had reached down and was rubbing my ears, so I was very distracted.

"NO!" I heard Andrew shout. "I don' want Bawbies; thay's for giwls."

"Well I don't want a baseball or a soccer ball or a football!" Amanda shouted back.

"If you can't decide without fighting, then you don't get anything," Omi warned.

It got very quiet. They started whispering again, and when I looked up, Amanda had a huge grin on her face, and Andrew was beaming. They came right up to Omi, and Amanda whispered something in her ear.

"Oh, that's a goot idea," said Omi. "But we

have to ask your parents if it's okay."

Andrew tore out of the room at the speed of light with Amanda right on his heals. I wanted to go after them and find out what they had decided on, but Omi picked me up just then.

"I wonder what you will think of their idea, hmm Charlie?" she asked.

"Meow." If you don't tell me what it is, how do I know?

Mom came out of the bedroom with a slightly irritated look on her face, but Amanda, Andrew, and Dad came out right behind her looking very pleased.

"Shall we go right now?" Dad asked.

"Okay by me," Omi said.

"All right!" shouted the kids, and they ran out the door.

"I'll wait here and get things ready," Mom said resignedly. Whatever this surprise was, Mom was not thrilled.

"You sure this is okay by you?" Omi asked her.

Mom smiled. "Yeah, I just know who is going to be taking care of everything by the end of the week."

Omi nodded knowingly and headed out after the kids.

Mom was looking at me. "Well Charlie," she said, "we'll see how we both do with this."

"Meow?" With WHAT?

They came home about an hour later. They were all carrying something. Dad had a big box in his arms, Omi had a little one, Amanda had a bag of what looked like sawdust in her hands, and Andrew had a box with some kind of seeds. Mom directed them to Andrew's room.

"Why Andrew's room?" Amanda demanded.

"Because Charlie sleeps in your room," Mom said, "and I'm not sure how he's going to react."

"Oh, yeah." Amanda looked startled, as if she hadn't given me a thought before this. "That could be a problem."

She stood looking at me for a moment, and then charged off into Andrew's room with the rest of them. I tried to follow, but she closed the door.

I waited by the door, looking under the crack below to see if I could tell what was going on. But all I could see were feet. There was a lot of rustling, some giggling, and then I heard Dad say, "Let's leave her alone for a while to settle in."

Her? HER? They wouldn't have brought home another cat without asking me, would they?

No, that didn't make sense. A kitten wouldn't

need sawdust, because it could use my litter box. And it wouldn't eat seeds.

A horrible thought came to me. NOT ANOTHER DOG! NO! I could handle Frisky now, but two of them? No way!

But wait, dogs don't eat seeds or sawdust. Just about everything else, but not seeds or sawdust. So what could it be?

As they all stepped out of Andrew's room, I zipped between some legs and ran in.

"Oh no, Charlie, not a chance," Dad said as he picked me up and carried me out. But before we left, I caught a glimpse of a cage on Andrew's dresser, and there was something small and furry in it.

Chapter 2

Rose

My name is Queen Rose. I am from a royal line of hamsters. I was born a princess, and since hamsters only live about two years, I am assuming my mother has passed on and left me as queen.

It had been quite a day for me. There I was, minding my own business, sleeping in a big pile of my brothers, sisters, and cousins in the pet store, when I suddenly saw this big face staring at me through the glass. Normally, this would have driven me crazy, being disturbed by people when I needed my royal nap. But this face was different. It was not as big as most people's, and the large blue eyes looking me over were so sweet. And I could tell he wasn't looking at all of us, he was just looking at me. When he saw me looking back, his smile was so huge that it seemed to take up most of his face.

What a sweet face, I thought, as I curled farther into the pile to go back to sleep. But then the roof opened. Uh-oh. The roof only opened for two reasons. It opened once a day for the cage to be cleaned and the food to be put in, but it wasn't that time of day. The only other time it opened was when a kidnapping was about to take place.

Kidnapping, you ask? Yes. Every so often, the roof would open, and a huge hand reached into our house and took one of us away, never to return. It was very frightening. So when a big hand reached in this time, I dove to the middle of the pile of my relatives. It became a swarming mass of fur and feet, as we all piled on top of each other and tried to claw our way to the bottom. I was very good at digging my way down; that was why the kidnappers had never gotten me before.

One by one, I could feel my brothers and sisters being move aside, as if they were looking for a specific one of us. In the past, the hand had always grabbed the first one it could reach, with some kind of comment like, "They all look alike anyway," echoing from the sky above. But this time, the hand kept digging.

"Is this the one?" the voice asked.

"No, dat one," a tiny voice said.

"Are you sure? They all look alike."

"No, it has to be dat one."

Oh no, I thought. Someone knows I'm the crown princess, and they're after me.

My suspicions were confirmed when the hand grabbed me, and the little voice rang out through the sky, "Dat's da one!"

I tried desperately to bite the hand that held

me so that it would open and I could escape.

"Ouch!" I heard the voice of the grabby hand say. "You sure you want this one? She's pretty vicious."

"Dat's da one," the little voice said. What a cute accent, I thought to myself. I wondered if he was the prince of some far off country. But before I could take another peek at him, I was shoved into a dark box, and the lid slammed closed.

Then I felt myself being jostled and bounced around. The box was being carried somewhere, but I couldn't tell what was going on. I could still hear voices outside, but they were muffled by the box, so I couldn't understand them. The bouncing stopped for a moment as if the box had been set down. Then I heard strange beeping noises, some papers moving around, and we started bouncing along again.

The box stopped, and more strange noises began. A loud motor was running somewhere nearby, and I had the strangest feeling that I was moving, but I knew the box was sitting still. The box lid opened just a tiny bit, and I could see those same blue eyes staring at me. I heard someone say, "Andrew, close that up! You don't want her to get loose in the car!" and the lid slammed closed again.

After a while, the motor sound stopped, and

the box and I resumed bouncing. I heard doors opening and closing, and we finally came to a stop that felt like I was on solid ground.

Some minutes later, the lid opened. I was ready. I had already figured that if I bit really hard into the first hand that grabbed me, it might drop me and I would run away and escape. If I could get away, maybe I could start a new empire, out in the wild, away from people. People, after all, were the cause of all my problems.

But the hand that reached into the box didn't try to grab me. It was tiny for a people hand, and it just rested on the floor in front of me, as if waiting for me to climb into it. Since I had no other way to get out of the box, I walked slowly into the hand.

A special kind of peace seemed to come over me the minute I stepped onto that hand. I settled down against it. The skin was soft and warm, very different from the fur of my brothers and sisters that I was used to cuddling against, but nice.

The hand carried me over and set me gently into a large cage. It was very nice from what I could see. It was made of a see-through material, so I could look out and observe three people looking at me. One was very large, one was small and had long fur on its head, and then there was the tiny one with the blue eyes. He was the one who had held me gently and made me feel so comfortable. I looked at him for a moment and wondered if he really was a prince.

"Let's leave her alone for a while and let her settle in," the big one said in a deep voice.

They all turned away then and started to leave the room. I was just beginning to admire my new surroundings, when I heard the deep voice again. "Oh no, Charlie, not a chance."

I looked quickly at the figures leaving the room. The big one was holding some kind of hairy, wild-eyed monster.

Chapter 3

Charlie

OKAY, THERE'S SOME KIND OF FURRY CREATURE in a cage in Andrew's bedroom. What could that mean? I tried to think.

I bet it's a treat for me. That's it. Omi doesn't know that I don't eat mice, and she thought she'd be really nice to me and get me a snack. Well, as much as I hated the thought of getting fur all over my tongue, I guessed I could eat it. Just to be nice.

Hmm, I wonder how juicy a mouse is. Will it be hard to catch? Will it put up a good fight? My mouth began to water in anticipation.

But wait. If that rodent in there was a gift for me, why did they get a cage, and food, and all the accessories?

Maybe they believed it was too skinny. Yeah, that's it. They must be fattening it up for me.

I grinned at the thought of a nice, fat mouse.

"Well," Mom's voice broke me out of my self induced trance, "how's the new pet settling in?"

Pet? Did she say pet? But, but, but . . . that's a rodent in there! Rodents aren't pets; they're pests! Oh, maybe I just heard her wrong.

"She's a little shaky right now, but I think she'll be fine," Dad answered.

"She's so soft, Mommy," Andrew said, "she feews wike a tiny kitty, like Chawie when he was wittle."

"Even softer," Amanda said.

"Meow!" Okay, we have a definite problem here. There is no way that any rodent is softer than I am. In fact, I don't like to be mentioned in the same sentence with a mouse, unless it is to describe how I caught one.

"Oh, sorry Charlie." Amanda again looked surprised to see me. "I didn't mean to hurt your feelings. The hamster is just a baby, so she'll probably lose some of her softness as she gets older, just like you did."

WHAT? Did she just compare me to a rodent again?

What did she call it? A hamster, not a mouse. I wondered what the difference was.

And why would anyone want to keep a

rodent as a pet? I mean, let's look at this logically. Rodents are too small to play with unless you aren't worried about squishing them. They're not pretty; in fact, they're downright ugly if you ask me. They shed, all they think about is food, you have to clean up after them constantly. . . .

Then again, except for the part about squishing them, I could say the same thing about dogs, and lots of people keep them as pets. I wonder if people are really as smart as I give them credit for.

Amanda sat down on the floor next to me and started petting me. She was trying to make up for saying insulting things, and I let her rub my ears. She has a way of rubbing my ears that makes me forget everything else. . . .

"What are you going to name your hamster?" I heard Omi ask.

"Her name is Wose," Andrew stated.

"Wose?" Amanda asked.

"No, Wose!" Andrew said.

"Why Wose?" Amanda wanted to know.

"Not Wose, Wose!" Andrew shouted.

"That's what I said, Wose!" Amanda yelled back.

"Wose, Wose, Wose!!" Andrew screamed.

"He's saying Rose," Mom calmly told Amanda.

"Oh," Amanda said as she rolled her eyes. "Okay, why Rose?"

"Because dat's her name." Andrew sounded exasperated.

"Well, how do you know that?" Amanda sounded irate.

"Because she tode me that was hew name."

"So, now you speak hamster?" Amanda asked in her most sarcastic voice.

"No, she didn't tell me wiff woids," Andrew said thoughtfully, "She just kinda . . . thought it to me."

"Yeah, right," Amanda said as she rolled her eyes again.

"Rose is a very nice name for her," Mom said sweetly, while giving Amanda a look that told her not to argue.

"Okay, Rose . . . Rose . . . Rosie . . . Rosie O'Hamster!" Amanda shouted.

Andrew giggled. "Wosie O'Hamster, dat's funny 'Manda."

"We better get going everybody," Dad said then. "We have to take Omi to the airport."

So the family grabbed all of Omi's things and headed for the garage. I felt sorry for them. They were sad because Omi was leaving, and they had a long car ride ahead of them. I hate car rides.

And on top of that, they now had a rodent for a pet. My poor family.

I went to talk to Frisky. Maybe being a stupid animal herself, she would have some insights into why people keep useless creatures as pets. Let's face it, cats are necessary. We add character, beauty, and grace to any home. We give love and comfort, and we listen patiently to all our people's problems. We keep pests out of the house.

Unless our people invite them in and stick

them into cages.

Frisky was out back, but I jumped up onto the windowsill and called to her through the open window. "Hey, Frisky!"

"What? Is something going on? Is anything wrong?" she asked in that totally dingy voice of hers. Typically clueless, I thought to myself.

"Nothing's wrong. I just wanted to talk to you."

"Oh," she answered. She tilted her head to one side and looked at me like talking was a totally foreign concept. "What's up? You don't usually want to 'just talk' unless something's bothering you."

Maybe she knew me better than I thought. "I'm having a hard time understanding something," I began. "Why do you think people keep pets? I mean, what are they thinking?"

Frisky's eyes got very big for a moment, and very blank. She began looking around, as if expecting the answer to be in the air somewhere around her. That's when I realized my mistake. I was asking about a concept that she had never mastered. Thinking.

"You can stop now," I said, as her eyes seemed to cross, "you have smoke coming out of your ears from trying to get that brain in gear." She just looked at me blankly again. One thing about Frisky, she never takes offense at an insult, because she never understands them. "What I wanted to tell you is this: Andrew has a new pet. It's a hamster."

"What's a hamster?" Frisky looked even more confused, if that's possible.

"It's something like a mouse, only I think it's a little bigger. I didn't get a real good look at it. But, why do you think they wanted another pet?"

"Maybe we're not doing a good job," she said sadly. Her head drooped down and her tail stopped wagging. "Maybe we just aren't good enough. Maybe they're looking for something we're not giving them. I try to do a good job, being a watchdog and loving them all and trying not to jump on them too much, but maybe I'm just not doing enough." She looked up at me with a suspicious glare. "And maybe you're not either."

"What do you mean by that?" I asked angrily.

"Maybe you're not giving them enough love, or letting them pet you enough, or whatever it is that a cat is supposed to do." She held that thought for one minute, then I could almost see it race right out of her brain as her mind switched to a different track. "What are cat's supposed to do anyway? Why do people keep cats as pets?" She seemed genuinely perplexed.

That was not even worth answering. If she hadn't figured out by now what superior creatures we cats are, she would never understand. "Forget it," I told her. "Just be aware that there's a new animal in the house, and you better not. . . ." I was about to warn her not to eat it, but stopped myself. There might come a time when I would want her to eat Rose. It would be pretty easy to convince Frisky that Rose was just another leftover that fell off the plate. I'd save that thought for the future, in case Rose turned out to be a problem.

Chapter 4

Rose

DAY TWO OF MY KIDNAPPING DRAMA. I was sleeping in the corner of the cage, in a pile of sawdust that took me hours to create. Long after the sweet giant named Andrew had closed his eyes in slumber on the other side of the room, I had circled the cage, looking for any means of escape. During the night, I had noticed furry paws reaching under the bedroom door trying to open it, so I knew the monster creature was trying to get me. No doubt he has murder on his mind, I thought with a shudder.

That's when I decided I had better hide myself before I went to sleep at dawn. So, I piled the wood chips, bit by bit, into one corner. Only when every chip in the cage had been stacked together could I allow myself to burrow deep into the pile and try to sleep. Ah, a bed fit for a queen. I had doubted that I would be able to sleep, being all alone in a strange place. But I was so tired from the emotional upheaval, and then all the work of creating my hidden bed, that I quickly drifted off to sleep in my pile of fluff.

Suddenly, I was being rudely awakened, yet again, by a giant hand picking me up out of my bed. What now? I wondered. Maybe it was time to send a ransom demand to my people. I wondered what they would ask for. Seeds? They had left plenty, in the bowl in my cage, so I doubted that was what they were after. Wood chips? Again, they seemed to have plenty. What else could my people possibly give them? Poop pellets? Well, we created plenty of those everyday as long as we ate well, and they were welcome to them. But perhaps they were valuable. After all, the keepers of the food that served us in the pet store had cleaned all the pellets away each day. Maybe they had great value to the giants. But what would they use them for? I didn't even want to think about it.

It became quickly apparent, though, that ransom was not the subject on the giant's mind at that moment. It was torture.

It was the Dad person's hand that held me,

but I could see my Andrew was at his side. They carried me across the room, until they came to a yellow ball sitting on a shelf. When they touched the ball, it opened, and I could see that it was actually a hollow sphere. Then, to my horror, they put me inside the sphere and closed it back up.

Now I was inside, surrounded by nothing but smooth, clear walls. I was relieved to find small holes in the sides that served to let fresh air in, so apparently this wasn't meant to be a tomb in which I would suffocate.

Hmm, this isn't so bad after all, I thought to myself. They carried me out of the small room and into the rest of the building. We came to a large area with a soft, sand-colored floor, lots of bright mountains (the giants call them 'furniture'), and a wall that looked out into the big, wide world. Being a night creature, the room seemed much too bright to me, so I kept my eyes half-closed as I was carried through. They took me right to the center of the big room, and the giant Dad sat me down in the middle of the floor.

The whole world looked yellow from inside the ball, and somehow that made it seem to be a very cheerful place. I could see the giants all standing around the room, watching me. They looked like they were expecting me to make a break for it, so I just continued to study my surroundings through partially closed eyes, rubbing my face every so often, as I do when I get nervous.

I was most interested in the wall that showed the outside world. That was where I wanted to be, out there, wild and free. I walked that direction, intending to put my hands on the side of the sphere to get a better look. But when I moved, the ball moved too! I tried again, and the ball inched closer to the wall. This was fabulous! I began to run, straight toward the opening, intending to break out and escape into the world.

"Looks like she's finally figured out her ball," I heard the Dad giant say.

"Yeah, but I think she's still got some things

to learn," the Mom answered.

I wasn't sure what that meant, but I was afraid they would figure out that I was trying to get away and would attempt to stop me, so I ran even faster.

Suddenly, BOOM! I hit the wall really hard, and the world went black.

Chapter 5

Charlie

WHEN DAD CARRIED THE YELLOW BALL into the living room, I thought that it was a new toy for me. Maybe he was trying to make up for the frustration I had gone through the night before.

At night, Andrew's door was normally open a crack, so Mom could hear him if he called out. I usually didn't bother to go in there, because I like to sleep on Amanda's bed, and Andrew tends to snore. But not wanting to go into a room and not being allowed to are very different things. Know how to make a cat really want to go someplace? Tell them it's a "no-no." I just wanted to get a good look at the hamster. I still hadn't figured out exactly what it was, or what affect it was going to have on our family. It didn't set well with me that the first thing she had done was to suddenly make one part of the house off-limits.

I could hear her moving around in there. All night long, I could hear her little feet moving across the newspaper and wood shavings. She was doing something in there, but I couldn't tell what. Was she setting up her house, or preparing for a party? I could picture her opening the bedroom window, inviting all the rodents in the neighborhood into the house, and them laughing at me, the cat who couldn't get in the room to catch them. When I started picturing the kind of housewarming presents the rodents would be bringing Rose, I realized I was getting hysterical and had better get some sleep.

I didn't get much rest, since Andrew woke Amanda up early in the morning, telling her she just had to, "Come and see da big bed Wosie made outta da wood stuff." Amanda had bounced out of bed, knocking me off in the process, then ran into Andrew's room and closed the door. Humph. What a way to start the day.

And now this big yellow ball was on the floor. I like balls. I really like the tiny ones, called super-balls. They roll all over the place, I can chase them just about anywhere, and they're light enough that when I catch one, I can toss it back up into the air and cause it to start rolling away again.

But this ball was really big. It was just about as tall as I am, and the yellow coloring was so bright that it kind of hurt my eyes to look at it. I wasn't sure it was going to be much fun to push around. Maybe it wasn't for chasing, like other balls. Amanda and I had watched a circus on TV one day, and they had these seals that walked around on top of great big balls. Maybe that was the idea, I was supposed to try to get on and ride it.

Hmm … I don't know. Cats are very graceful, and I'm no exception, but we also don't like to be caught doing something that isn't smooth and elegant. And for some reason, the whole family was standing around, watching the

ball, like they were waiting for me to do something with it.

I walked up to the ball very slowly. It was still kind of hard to look at it, but maybe if I carefully put my paws on top of it, one at a time, I could climb on without having to stare at it. Just as I reached out to put my first paw on the ball, it suddenly moved.

MOVED! How does a ball move by itself? I took a step closer to the ball, and it moved again! I heard Dad's voice behind me, "Looks like she's finally figured her ball out."

"Yeah, but I think she's still got some things to learn," Mom answered.

Suddenly, the ball flew into the back door. BOOM! It hit the glass really hard and just stopped.

"Ouch, that must've hurt," I heard Amanda say.

Okay, why is she worried about the ball's feelings?

Andrew ran up to the ball. "She's otay," he said happily.

I didn't have much time to wonder what that meant, because the ball backed up a few inches, and then slammed itself into the door again.

"I wonder if we should put her away for a while," Mom said.

I started laughing. I couldn't help myself. The whole situation was just too weird to do anything but laugh. I mean, you've got this big, bright colored ball, wandering around the room by itself, slamming into glass doors, and my people are worried about it getting hurt and referring to it as a girl. It was way too bizarre.

Suddenly, I stopped laughing. The ball was coming toward me. Slowly at first, then faster and faster, until it was about to crash into me. I jumped back, startled by this change in events. The ball kept coming at me, barreling in my direction as if it wanted to run me over. So, I did what any self-respecting animal would do in the same situation. I ran!

Mom and Dad were laughing, I could hear them. Amanda was giggling, and Andrew was just standing there with his mouth hanging open, as the yellow ball began chasing me across the living room and into the kitchen. They continued to just watch and laugh, getting louder and louder, as I ran faster and faster. What is the matter with them? I thought. A ball is chasing me, and they're cracking up!

"Meow!" I yelled. Hey, I need a little help here!

"This is too much," Mom laughed. "We better rescue Charlie," she said sarcastically.

About time! Hello, I'm running from a ball here!

Amanda came over and picked me up. Safe at last.

Suddenly Andrew seemed to come to his senses. "That's not vewy nice. Wosie, stop chasin' Chawlie."

Andrew walked over and picked up the ball. He twisted one side, and it seemed to come apart.

Good, I thought. He killed the ball. It will never chase me again.

Andrew reached his hand inside the ball, then started to pull his hand back out again. I watched closely. I'd never seen ball guts before, and I wondered what they might look like.

But when his hand came out, it had the hamster in it. How did . . . but I thought . . . what in the . . . huh?

Then it came to me. Rose had been inside the ball, controlling it. No wonder the family had been laughing so hard. They had just watched their cat run away from a hamster.

Chapter 6

Rose

W<small>HEN</small> I <small>WOKE UP</small>, I was dizzy and still slightly dazed. Through the yellow sphere, I could see the face of my Andrew, smiling and happy that I had opened my eyes.

"Shc's otay," I heard him say.

I was right next to the opening in the wall. I could see the great outdoors and freedom. I backed the ball up a few inches, looked around to make sure no one would try to stop me, and ran forward again.

SLAM!

Okay, something was in the way. Something I couldn't see. No wonder they hadn't tried to stop me. Apparently, they had an invisible force field blocking the way!

So, escape could not come from that exit. I

would have to find another way out.

As I collected my wits and looked around the room, I noticed the monster coming toward me. He looked even more sinister through the yellow haze that surrounded me.

As he approached, instead of hunger, I noticed curiosity in his eyes. This might be a chance for me to convince him that I was not a snack to be messed with.

I started rolling toward him very slowly. When I saw surprise and then fear in his eyes, I started running straight at him.

I'm not sure what I was expecting, but when he turned around and started running away from me, I kept after him. He ran faster. I ran faster. He kept going from room to room, and I stayed right on his trail. I was beginning to get tired, but I was also gaining on him. Maybe if I ran over his tail a few times he would know not to mess with Queen Rose.

I was just about at the tip of his tail when he somehow flew up into the air and out of my reach. I mean, one moment he was there, the next he was gone. I was so busy trying to figure out what had happened that I almost ran into a wall.

Then I saw him. He was in the arms of the giant girl.

Drat! So the monster had an ally. I would have to watch out for this 'Amanda' person.

Andrew picked up the ball at that moment, pulled me out and put me right next to his mouth. "That's not vewy nice. Wosie, stop chasin Chawlie." Then he put me back into the sphere and set it on the floor.

I spent the next few minutes walking around the house in my sphere. I started thinking of it as my private bubble, from which I could survey the world while being protected from it. I never found another opening to the outside, at least, not one that

I could reach. There were some, way up in the air, but from the strange reflections I could see on them, they all had force fields too.

Some time later, Prince Andrew came and picked up my bubble and carried me back to the prison. But now I knew the layout of the house. A plan was beginning to form in my mind. The giants had left their home before, when they kidnapped me. Eventually, they would leave again, and when they did, they would have to let down the force fields to get out. I would be ready.

Chapter 7

Charlie

HUMILIATION. There was no other word for what I was feeling. I mean, letting myself be chased by some over-sized mouse?

Amanda had carried me back to her bedroom. I was so embarrassed that I was probably bright pink beneath my fur. I tried to hide under the bed, but Amanda held me to her chest and began to pet me.

"It's okay, Charlie," she spoke softly into my ear. "It was very mean of Rose to do that to you. I'd run if a giant ball chased me, too."

My tail jumped back up to attention. Well, of course I had nothing to be ashamed of. Anyone else would have done the same thing. With my dignity intact, I stayed with Amanda and let her pet me. I wouldn't admit, even to myself, that I was purposely not leaving the room until Rose was back in her cage. I would be perfectly happy if I never had to see that rodent again.

When I heard Andrew's bedroom door close, I knew Rose was back where she belonged. I hoped that everyone else in the family had the same attitude Amanda did, and I wouldn't need to worry about them making fun of me.

Except when I walked into the kitchen and looked at Dad; he started cracking up. And when I looked out the back door, Frisky took one look at me and burst out laughing.

Dignity intact. Yeah, right.

I probably could have lived with the memory of my embarrassment and eventually forgiven and forgotten the whole affair. But when Rose hurt my Amanda, she crossed the line of no return.

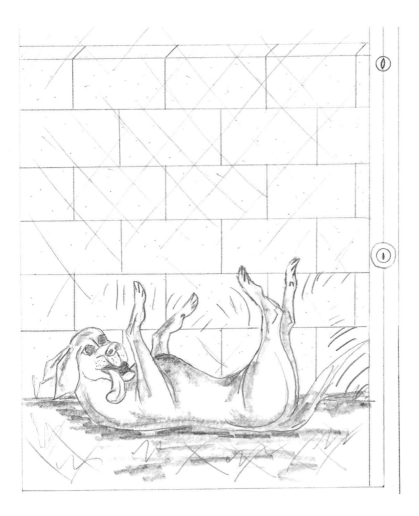

Chapter 8

Rose

LIFE REALLY WASN'T BAD AS A HOSTAGE. The food was even better than at the pet store, I had the whole cage to myself instead of having to share it with thirty or so other hamsters, the bedding was soft and clean, and Prince Andrew was wonderful company.

I also had this marvelous round thing in my cage. It was made of shiny metal, and when I stepped into it, it would move with me. I could run, and it would turn in circles so that I stayed in the same place, even if I ran as fast as I could. Isn't that fascinating? I could run and run and run, and then if I suddenly stopped, I would go swinging backwards! It was so exciting!

The next few days I worked on devising my escape plan. I spent hours and hours, circling my

cage, looking for any edge, any crack, any possible
way to get out. I spun in my wheel for long peri-
ods of time, envisioning the whole plan.

Once out of my cage, I would sneak quietly across the dresser. I would jump onto
Andrew's bed from there; the cloth looked soft
enough to break my fall. That cloth went all the
way to the floor, so I could easily climb down.
Once on the ground, I would scurry to the bedroom door. The crack underneath was only
about an inch high, but I could smash myself
down to fit under (another reason to continue
running on the wheel and keep all that seed from

going to my hips). Then I would go straight to the big room with the invisible door. With any luck, the giants would leave the force field down while they were gone, and I would escape into the great outdoors. Then I would find the pet store (it couldn't be too far away, could it?), let my family out of the big cage, and start a new kingdom out in the wild. My subjects would adore me more than ever, and they would do whatever I asked to make our new realm the greatest land on earth. I would call it, "Hamsterdam."

There was only one possible problem with my escape plan. The monster. But I didn't think he would be too much of a problem. For one thing, he seemed to sleep a great deal. I don't know if all of his kind do, but this particular monster seemed to be sleeping sixteen hours a day, at least from what I could figure out by listening to the rest of the family. I would just have to make sure he was asleep when I made my run for freedom.

Besides, if he was awake, I could handle him. All I'd have to do was run right at him. He seemed to be scared to death of me. I am one tough hamster, I thought with pride.

One afternoon, as I was sleeping peacefully under my pile of wood shavings, I heard the bedroom door open. I carefully opened one eye to see what was going on. It was the giant girl, and she was coming toward the cage.

She was creeping silently along, as if she were afraid of getting caught at whatever it was she had in mind. Why, she's as sneaky as that monster she's friends with, I thought to myself. I stayed perfectly still and pretended to be asleep as she quietly opened the cage and reached inside.

"Hi Rose. I just wanted to come and see you and hold you for a little while." She was whispering sweet words to me. Trying to lull me into a false sense of security, no doubt.

But I knew the truth. You can't hang out with monsters and not learn to be like them. She was probably planning on taking me to that creepy thing, then feeding me to him as a gesture of friendship. I was not going to let that happen.

I let her move her hand all the way under me, until I was cupped in her palm, with her fingers right in front of me. I continued to pretend I was asleep until she started lifting me up. Then I sunk my two big front teeth into her.

"OUCH!" She screamed and dropped me back into the cage. I smiled to myself as she ran out of the room crying. Let the monster know, I thought to myself, that I am not going to be lunch anytime soon. If he ever does get ahold of me, he'll have a fight on his hands. I'll bite and scratch for everything I'm worth. I will survive, no matter what it takes.

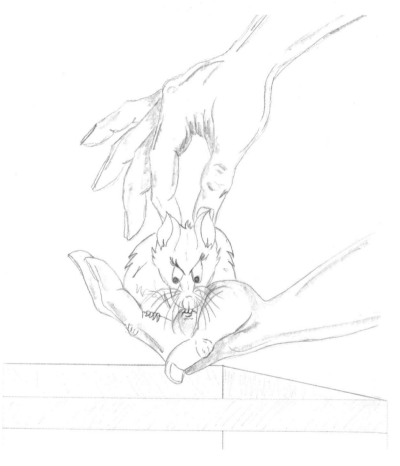

Chapter 9

Charlie

I WAS TAKING MY MID-AFTERNOON NAP on Amanda's bed, when suddenly I could hear her crying. She was running down the hall toward the kitchen, and I raced out of the bedroom to find out what was wrong even before my eyes were fully open. She was screaming for Mom, who came running from wherever she had been to see what had happened.

Amanda was bleeding. Mom was carrying her to the kitchen and grabbing a washcloth to stop the blood and clean up the wound. I wondered what had happened. Had she fallen on something sharp? Had she been playing with something that was dangerous?

As she began to calm down, Mom finally got her to stop crying and answer those important questions. "It's okay now honey," she said quietly, "but I need you to tell me how this happened, so I know how much it has to be cleaned."

"IT WAS ROSE!" Amanda practically screamed. "She bit me! I just tried to pick her up. I was being very gentle, the way Daddy told us, and she bit me really hard!" She started crying again.

"Why did you go in there by yourself?" Mom asked. "Why didn't you ask Andrew if it was okay to go into his room, and why didn't you tell me what you were going to do?"

"I was afraid Charlie would be upset if he saw me with Rose," Amanda said sheepishly. "If I asked, Charlie might have heard me, and then his feelings would have been hurt."

"I see," Mom replied. "Well, you're not hurt badly, because it's not very deep; it just seems bad because this part of your hand bleeds a lot if it gets punctured. Let's clean it up really well, though, so we don't have to worry about it getting infected."

They walked into the bathroom, and Mom took out a bottle of "The Stingy Stuff," as Amanda and Andrew call it. Andrew and I were standing in the doorway watching, so Mom closed the door. We looked at each other as Amanda let out another yell and started crying again.

"I guess Wosie has some shawp teef," Andrew said in an awed voice. I guess the idea that the little rodent was dangerous had never occurred to him.

I was furious. How dare she? How dare she hurt

my Amanda? Didn't she know that Amanda was the sweetest, most amazing person in the whole world? She should have been honored that Amanda wanted to spend time with her. The fact that she was trying to spare my feelings in the matter only made me even angrier. Amanda had been willing to give a little of her wonderful affection to that stinky little furball, and it attacked her?!

I walked over to Andrew's bedroom door. It was closed, but I snarled underneath, loud enough so the rodent would be sure to hear. "You are now officially warned. I will get you back for this, Hamster. Some way, some how, you will pay for hurting my girl. Be aware. Be on the look-out. I will find a way to make sure you regret ever having even thought about messing with Amanda," I growled.

I was so angry, and I just didn't know what to do. I was not used to having all these terrible thoughts, these mean feelings. I kept picturing different ways I was going to get Rose. I imagined eating her, sharpening my claws on her, playing baseball with her (she was the ball), growling at her so fiercely that she had a heart attack. . . .

I had to find a way to get these awful images out of my brain so I could think calmly and rationally. Then I would figure out what I would really do to her.

I waited until I knew Amanda was okay, and then I went to the back door and asked to go out. I needed some fresh air.

Frisky was in the house, so I didn't have to try to explain what I was feeling to her. She had looked just as shocked as Andrew had when she saw what Rose had done. I walked over and hopped on top of the fence. Maybe if I were closer to heaven, I might be able to get rid of these nasty feelings.

"Hey Charlie, what's up man?" I heard a deep, heavily accented voice ask.

I looked down and saw Pepe. Pepe is the Chihuahua that lives next door, and we became friends the first time we met. This was despite the fact that he was a dog, and a really funny looking dog at that.

"Hi Pepe."

"How's my little angel doin' today?" he asked.

"Frisky's okay," I answered. Pepe was in love with Frisky, and the feeling was mutual. The problem was that Pepe thought Frisky was some cute, little pooch, when in fact she was a good-sized Labrador. And somehow he had gotten the impression that she was very intelligent, which I couldn't quite figure out, since he talked to her through the fence everyday.

On the other hand, Frisky thought Pepe was some big, strong, Latin-lover type. If they ever met, they would both be sadly disappointed, so I didn't bother to correct their ideas about each other. Let them be in love. It was better than hate, which was what I was currently feeling.

"Pepe, have you ever heard of a hamster?"

"Is that the kinda meat they put in burritos?"

"No, it's a kind of pet people keep. Kind of like a mouse, only bigger."

"Choo mean like a rat? Rats are very bad,

man. If you talkin' about some kinda rat, I don' wanna hear it."

"No Pepe, it's not a rat. Andrew just got one a few days ago." I sat down on top of the fence. "It was bad enough that they brought the thing into the house, but now it bit my Amanda. What should I do?"

"Why don' choo just eat it?" Pepe asked. "I thought cats liked to eat mouses."

"I don't," I shivered at the thought. "All that fur. The thought makes me sick."

"Well, when there's somethin' that's really buggin' me, I jus' bite it. Choo know? Just bite it, and bite it and bite it. . . ." He was ripping at the air as he spoke, tearing some invisible enemy apart. I almost laughed, but I was too miserable to try.

"I'd still end up with a mouthful of fur," I interrupted him. "Besides, Andrew likes the stupid thing, and he might get mad at me."

"What choo care about that for? After all, didn't choo say he was the one that brought the stu-pid thing home?"

He had a point. "Thanks Pepe. I don't know if I can bring myself to bite her, though."

"Just pretend she's a taco. Or a tostada. Or an encharito. . . ." He was so busy thinking about food that he almost forgot I was there. Suddenly he shook his head. "I gotta stop thinking about food, and get back to guarding the house. It's almost dark, and there's a burglar in the 'hood, man."

"There's a what?" I asked, not believing my ears.

"Choo heard me. There's some kinda thief in the area. I heard some of the other dogs barkin' about it. Seems like they broke into about five houses man, and they stole all the good stuff that was inside. The thought of someone getting into my 'frigerator and stealin' my food. . . ."

"Pepe, if someone's going to break in, they aren't going to steal food. I heard burglars steal TVs and stuff like that."

"Show's what choo know, man. Who cares about stuff like that?" He got a silly grin on his face. "Besides, you should be nervous Charlie. I heard this guy is a 'cat' burglar!" He started laughing at his own joke.

"Ha, ha, very funny Pepe. But what are you going to do if you actually see a burglar, gnaw at his ankles? That's about all you could reach!" I can be just as sarcastic as he can.

"That's not funny, man. I would bark at him, and then jump and bite him everywhere. I'd pretend he was a taco, and that'd be the end of that bad guy's career, let me tell you!" With that, he put a mean sneer on his face and began to pace back and forth across his yard.

I decided to head over to the Kit-Cat Club. That's the local blues place where the neighborhood cats all hang out. I thought I could talk to a few of them and see if anyone else had ever faced this problem before. And my friend Blackie would probably be there. He's older and wiser than I am, so maybe he could help.

As I climbed through the hole in the hedge that served as the door to the club, I heard someone calling my name. "Hey, Charlie!"

I turned around and saw Blackie right behind me. "I was just on my way to see you," I said.

"And I was just on my way to join the band," Blackie said. Blackie is a great blues singer. He has that kind of low, raspy voice that's just made for jazz. "Feel like jamming with us, Charlie? You look like you've got the blues for sure today."

"You've got that right," I agreed. Then the idea for a song hit me, and I realized it would be a good way to get my problem heard by the whole crowd at once. After I was done singing, I could sit down at one of the tables (they were actually just overturned planters) and anyone with answers could come over and talk to me. "Let's get to the stage!" I said enthusiastically.

There were probably twenty or more cats sitting around the club, and they all started cheering as Blackie and I walked up to the stage. We both smiled and waved, and I told the band the song I had in mind. Blackie picked up his mini saxophone, the piano player put his paws to the keys, and the drummer picked up her sticks. They waited for the signal from me, which I gave as I started to sing:

My family got a hamster,
and it's giving me a pain;
the thought of eating it keeps
flashing through my brain.
But my friend Andrew,
he likes this ball of fur;
and it would hurt him,
if I were to hurt her.

I'm gagging on this problem,
like a hairball in my throat.
I'd like to send her out to sea,
In a leaky little boat.

This stupid little rodent is
giving me the blues;
I wish she'd disappear, like
yesterday's news.
So Andrew buddy, would your
feelings be too 'ruffed,
if I get rid of her, and
get you one that's stuffed?

I'm gagging on this problem,
like a hairball in my throat. Yeah.
She really better be nice,
or I'll turn her into a coat.

The applause was deafening, as cats scratched the pottery tables with their claws to show their approval. I went down to a table by myself, as Blackie and the band continued to play.

Several cats came over to talk to me, but no one seemed to know what to do with a rodent other than eat it. After a while, I started to feel depressed, which was worse than being angry, so I decided to go home. It was already getting late, and maybe some dinner would improve my mood.

As long as it was cat food and not hamster.

Chapter 10

Frisky

HUH? WHAT?

(*Note to readers:* Sorry about that. Since Charlie and Rose are both getting to tell their side of this story, I thought it would be nice for Frisky to add something. So I asked her to tell me what she thought about the whole situation, about what's inside her head. As usual, there was nothing.)

Chapter 11

Rose

I HAD A STRANGE FEELING IN MY STOMACH, and it had been there all day. At first, I thought maybe I had food poisoning from biting the girl, then I remembered I hadn't actually taken a bite of her, but I had just bitten into her. The feeling seemed to grow worse and worse as the day wore on, and it began to travel from the pit of my stomach up to my heart. Every time I thought about how the little girl had cried, it hurt even worse. I tried running on my wheel, around and around, for hours on end, but the feeling wouldn't go away.

Finally I stopped running and went to lie down. Now I was tired, sweaty, and my stomach still hurt. That's when I heard the voice.

"You know what the problem is."

I looked around, but no one was in the room.

"Who said that?" I asked.

"It's me, your conscience," the voice stated.

"My what?"

"Your conscience. You know, the part of you that makes you feel guilty when you do something wrong."

"I don't think so," I explained. "You see, royalty never has to feel guilty. My mother told me that. Besides, if I had a conscience, I think I would have heard from it before now."

"You've never done anything this rotten before," the voice answered.

Suddenly I saw something standing on my shoulder. It looked a lot like me, only much smaller and with little wings sticking out of its back. I jumped up and ran to the other side of the cage, but the little hamster came with me.

"It's okay." That same voice that had been talking before came out of the little thing's mouth. *"It's just me. I thought maybe you'd believe me more if you could see me."*

"I don't understand. How can you be me, and be floating there next to me?" I asked.

"You have much bigger things to worry about," the winged me stated. *"How's your stomach feeling?"*

"Worse than ever. Are you the one making

me feel bad?"

"No, that's you."

"But you said you are me."

"Well . . . okay, so maybe I am the part of you that's making you feel sick, but that's because of what you did, not what I did."

"Huh?" I was becoming very confused.

"Let's just stick to the facts, shall we?" the little me continued. *"You bit that girl, and now you feel guilty."*

"But I've never felt guilty before."

"I already covered that. You've never done anything this bad before."

I thought about that. I had always been a very well behaved little hamster, even though I was a princess. Mother had made it very clear that I had to set an example for all the other little hamsters if I wanted to rule over them someday. But I had a good reason for what I had done.

"Why would I feel guilty for hurting one of my captors?"

"Because they have never hurt you. Even though they took you from your family and put you in a cage, they really have been nothing but kind to you. Except for exposing you to that, that, creature, they have actually treated you nicer than you have ever been treated before."

I thought about it. These giants had kidnapped me. I still couldn't understand why they had taken me, or what they wanted, but I did know one thing. Prince Andrew was not an evil person. He would never hurt me.

But I had hurt someone.

"Doesn't being royal make me exempt from feeling bad about stuff like this?" I finally asked.

"No," the little me answered. *"No one is exempt from feeling bad when they treat others like they are less than rodent. You wouldn't have done that to another hamster, so you shouldn't do it to a people."* With that, she disappeared.

It was late at night when I heard the monster come home. He had to stand outside the back door, yowling his head off until the Mom woke up and let him in.

The door to Prince Andrew's room was open a crack. Usually he kept it closed so the monster couldn't get in, but I guess he'd forgotten and left it open a bit. I saw the creature walk by, and he stopped to stare in through the door.

I don't think he would have come in if I hadn't called to him. He had already turned away when I spoke. "May I talk to you for a moment?" I asked quietly.

He seemed to think that he had imagined my talking to him, because he kind of shook his head and just continued to stare. "Please," I tried again, "I really need to ask you something."

He walked right up to the cage and stared at me. I backed away from the glass, all the way to the other side of the cage. He really was huge compared to me. When he opened his mouth to speak, all I could see were his teeth. "What do you want?" he growled.

"First of all, I'm sorry about the little girl," I paused there. I had never apologized for anything in my life, and I expected that he would be shocked and overwhelmed by my doing so. Instead, he just continued to stare at me. "Ah, well, anyway. . . ." I wasn't quite sure how to continue. Finally I just blurted out, "I'm confused. Why are these people being nice to me when they kidnapped me? Or why did they kidnap me just to be nice to me? Why am I here? What do they want? What does it all mean?!" I was shouting by the time I finished.

"Kidnapped? Who said you were kidnapped? How in the world did you get that idea?"

"They took me from my home, from my family. What else could it be?"

"What are you talking about?" the monster replied.

"I don't know why I'm here," I said sadly.

He looked at me like I was some weird bug that he had never seen before. "You're a pet. Just like me, just like Frisky. What's so confusing about that?"

"What's a pet?" I asked.

He gave me that strange look again. "Are you serious? You really don't know what a pet is, or why you're here with Andrew?"

"No."

He didn't laugh, like I thought he might. He just continued to stare at me for another moment, then turned and left the room.

He wasn't at all helpful, but at least he didn't eat me.

Chapter 12

Charlie

I DON'T KNOW ABOUT YOU, but when I need to do some serious thinking, there's no place like under a bed. My bed of choice is Amanda's. It's very quiet under there, and no one walking by is going to step on you by accident. Amanda stores some stuff under there. She has a suitcase full of dress-up clothes, some paper doll books, and there are usually some extra things like halves of plastic Easter eggs, a sock or two, and an old slipper. It's a little dusty, and sometimes cramped, but no one bothers me, and it gives me a chance to think. I had some important thinking to do.

My talk with the rodent had been enlightening. She was confused, but seeing as I deal with Frisky every day, I can handle that. The fact that she thought she had been kidnapped was just too bizarre. I mean, who would kidnap an oversized mouse? Why would they? If I hadn't been so surprised by the idea, I would have laughed in her face. I wished I had.

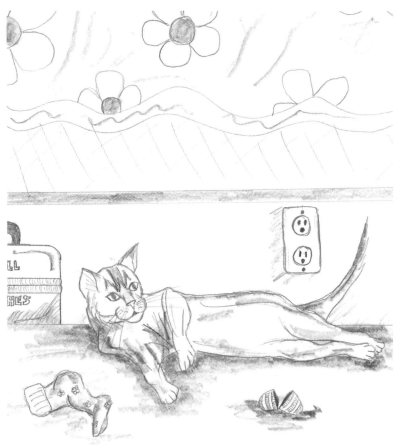

But then she had asked me what a pet was. That was the same question I had been asking all day. It depressed me to think that I didn't know the answer. I should be smart enough to figure it out, right?

It would have driven me crazy at that moment if I had realized Rose would be the one who ended up explaining it to me.

That was probably the scariest day of my life, and if you know me, that's saying a lot. I've faced street gang cats, a killer dog, and a coyote, but nothing was as bad as seeing one of my people hurt.

It was a normal afternoon. Dad was at work; Amanda had just gotten home from school. Mom was back in her bedroom cleaning the closet. I'd had a great afternoon playing in the clothes, boxes, hats, scarves and everything else she had pulled out of there. I was taking a break (actually Mom had chased me out of the room), and Amanda and I were watching TV.

Andrew was supposed to be taking a nap. That's where he had been for the last hour, and he hadn't told anyone or made any noise when he got up. Instead, he had snuck into the kitchen and was going to make himself a snack. He went through all the cupboards until he found exactly what he wanted; his favorite fruit in the whole world, pineapple. The pineapple was in a can, but it had a pull-open top, so he decided to open it.

Of course, we weren't there when this happened. I put it all together later, after we heard the screaming.

I've never seen Mom run so fast. But I'd never heard a cry of pain like that before, either. Amanda and I froze for a moment, and then ran toward the kitchen ourselves.

When we got there, Mom already had Andrew in her arms and a towel wrapped around his hand. The pineapple can was sitting there, half opened, with blood on the rim. The towel wrapped around his hand was already turning red, so I guessed he must have cut himself really badly.

Mom told Amanda, who was standing in the middle of the floor trying not to cry, to get the car keys. Amanda grabbed Mom's purse, Mom scooped Andrew up, and the three of them ran out to the car. Mom was telling Amanda to call Dad on the cell phone, so that he could meet them at the hospital.

It wasn't until I turned around that I realized Andrew had let Rose out before he went to make his snack.

Chapter 13

Rose

I HAD SEEN EVERYTHING. My beloved Andrew had awoken me when he finished his nap and had put me in my yellow sphere to get some exercise. I had followed him to the cabinet room. That was what I called it, because all of the walls seemed to be covered in doors. They weren't doors big enough for the giants to walk through, which seemed kind of strange, until I realized they had food and other things hidden behind each door. Oh, how I would love to wander around in there! I thought to myself. I could gather enough food for my entire kingdom to live on for a year, without having to go through more than one door. Of course, I'd have to figure out how to carry it all. . . .

That's what I was thinking about when I heard my Andrew scream. He was hurt! I didn't know

exactly what was wrong, but my heart cried just looking at him and hearing his moans of pain. When I bit
the Amanda girl, she had been hurt, but after a minute,
the blood and the crying had both stopped. Andrew
kept crying and bleeding. The Mom person was there
right away, and she seemed to know what to do, but
my Andrew was still sobbing, and the Mom actually
seemed worried. It was only a few seconds later that
they ran from the room, and I was left alone.

But not alone. The monster came walking

around the corner a few moments later, and seemed startled to see me. I considered chasing after him again, scaring him as I had before. I started rolling slowly in his direction.

"I'm not falling for that again," he said as I approached. "I can't see you very well, but I know you're in there.

"Don't look so scared," he continued, "I'm too worried to eat you right now, even if I wanted to."

I thought maybe if I changed the subject, then I could keep his mind off eating, especially off eating me. "Why are you so worried?" I asked.

"It's Andrew. He looked really hurt, and I'm very anxious about him."

"Do you think he was hurt that badly?" I asked, suddenly even more upset.

"They took him to the hospital. I've seen hospitals on TV. They're very big places where people go when they're in bad shape. It's like the vet, only much worse. Sometimes people die in hospitals," he said in a very small voice.

My Andrew, at the people's vet? I knew what a vet was. Sometimes the vet would come to the pet store to give shots to other animals. Sometimes, when the animals got sick, they would leave with the vet and never come back. Would Andrew never come back?

As we both sat there worrying, we heard a strange sound. Someone was trying to open the front door, but they didn't seem to have a key.

Chapter 14

Charlie

SOMEONE WAS TRYING TO BREAK INTO THE HOUSE. I looked around for Frisky, so she could bark at whoever it was and scare him away. I ran around the house, frantically searching, but Frisky was locked in the backyard. Great, there was only me and the hamster to protect the house.

I ran back to the front room just in time to see the door begin to shake.

"What's going on?" Rose asked me. "Why are you running around like a lunatic? Or is that normal for you?"

"Someone is trying to rob the house!" I yelled. "We have to stop him!"

"Why? What does 'rob' mean?"

"It means that the person who is coming

through that door is a bad man. He wants to take
our family's things. Our people will be really
sad if that happens," I explained.

"This person is going to do something that
would make Andrew even sadder? After everything that has happened to him today, this person
wants to make it worse?" Rose asked in a
shocked voice.

I suddenly had another thought. "Oh no! What if it's the cat burglar? He might try to steal me!" I ran across the room and went behind one of the big chairs. That way I could see the door, but the burglar wouldn't notice me.

I could see that Rose was only about ten feet away from the door as the lock suddenly gave, and the door swung open. . . .

Chapter 15

Rose

THE MONSTER WAS HIDING behind a big blue mountain, as the burglar person came creeping through the door. The big coward. He was going to leave it up to me to stop this bad person.

The man was dressed all in black, and he had a hat pulled low over his face so I couldn't really see him. As he slowly walked into the room, he looked down and saw me, then continued walking. I guess he wasn't aware that I was a queen, so he didn't know he was missing the most valuable item in the house. As he walked toward the living room, he left the front door wide open.

Now was my chance. Freedom was only ten feet away. Obviously, the Mom forgot to

86

turn the force field on when she left in such a hurry, or the man wouldn't have been able to walk right through it.

I could make a run for it. I would go out the door, somehow get out of the yellow ball, and find a beautiful meadow. Once I had found a nice, sandy home, I could make my way back to the pet store and free my family. Then we could start our new kingdom, and I would be the adored ruler of generations of hamsters.

I revved up my feet, ready to make a mad dash for freedom. But as I looked toward the door, I saw the burglar again. He looked so evil, all dressed in black. A plan began to form in my mind, a way to stop him from hurting my family. But it would mean giving up on my plans for escape.

Then I realized what I had done. I had called these people "my family." I thought about my sweet Andrew, how wonderful he was to me, and how safe he made me feel. The idea of leaving and never seeing him again. . . .

I suddenly changed direction. Instead of running for the door, I veered to the left, just as the burglar was about to pass me. I rolled under his feet at the perfect moment to send him falling on his face.

I wasn't sure what to do next. The man was lying on the floor, but he was about to get up again. That's when the cat jumped in. He leapt out from behind the chair and landed claws first on the burglars back.

Chapter 16

Charlie

WHEN ROSE STARTED RUNNING TOWARD THE BURGLAR, I wasn't sure what she was up to. But when he went falling to the ground, I realized that she was trying to help.

I remembered when I first met Dad. At the time, I hadn't meant to hurt him, but I didn't know how to control my claws. This time I knew exactly how to use them as weapons, and how to inflict the most damage.

I ran across the room and jumped on the bad guy's back. He shrieked in pain as all twenty claws dug into him.

He jumped up and was about to come after me when Rose ran into his feet from the backside, and he lost his balance. This time he fell on his rear end, and I ran in and clawed up and down both of his arms in about ten seconds, then dashed out of reach before he could grab me. He sat there screaming and was looking for me when Rose backed up and rammed into him again. As he turned to stop her, I leaped over the top of his head, dragging my claws across his skull in the process.

"This is nuts! Forget it, I'll go next door instead," the burglar yelled as he ran out the door, slamming it behind him. But apparently he had made too much noise while he was fighting with us. I heard a siren outside and ran to the window just in time to see a police car stop in front of our house, and an officer grabbed the thief as he tried to get away.

"We did it Rose! We stopped him!" I turned to look at the yellow ball on the floor.

She was sitting in the center of the circle, just staring at me with those beady black eyes. She seemed as surprised as I was that we had cooperated to get rid of the burglar.

"Why didn't you run?" I asked her. "You said they 'kidnapped' you. The door was open, and no one was going to stop you. Why didn't you escape?"

"If that bad person had taken things, it would have made my prince sad," she answered.

"Your prince?"

"You know," she said, "Prince Andrew."

She cared about Andrew. She was still delusional, living in a fantasy world of her own, but she cared about Andrew.

I was beginning to like her, in spite of myself. Scary.

A little while later, Mom brought Andrew and Amanda back. Andrew had a big bandage on his hand and he was really sleepy, but he was going to be okay. As Mom walked through the door, she looked surprised. "Oh my goodness," she said, "we left the front door unlocked! It's a good thing no one tried to break in."

I looked at Rose, and we both smiled.

Chapter 17

Rose

BY THE TIME I WAS BACK IN MY CAGE that afternoon, it was almost time for me to be waking up for the night, so I didn't bother to go back to sleep. It had been a revealing day, and I had a lot to think about.

He could have eaten me. He had the opportunity before the evil man showed up. I had no doubt that he could have opened the ball and got me. So why hadn't he? And why had he seemed so surprised when I told him I stayed for Andrew? Andrew and I are meant to be together; anyone can see that. Or could they? I guess I hadn't realized it myself until I saw him in pain. Now, he meant more to me than anything or anyone. Why, I'd even give up my kingdom for him, if I had to.

And I had. As I thought about all my plans, my kingdom in the country with my family and all my royal subjects worshipping me, I realized that those things weren't important anymore. I would rather spend time with Andrew than with a hundred loyal hamsters.

Andrew came in to talk to me before he went to bed. "I'm sowwy, Wosie," he said sweetly. "If Chawlie had eaten you when I left you in your ball, I would have been weally sad."

Me too. I reached my front paws up on the side of the glass cage to get closer to him. Andrew put one of the fingers from his unhurt hand up against the glass and touched where my paws were. It was like snuggling, and I liked it.

Charlie came into the room after it was very late. I had just been sitting by the edge of the cage, watching Andrew. I was still a little worried about him after his accident. The cat stopped about a foot away from the cage and laid down, which was nice because it meant I didn't have to look up to talk to him. "So you care about Andrew, huh?" he asked me.

"Of course. He's the most wonderful person in the whole world," I answered.

"Well, one of the most wonderful. The rest of the family are pretty nice, too," he said.

I thought about that. "I really don't know the others yet, but I guess if they're Andrew's family, they must be nice."

"Then why did you bite Amanda?" he asked in a voice that said he still hadn't forgiven me yet.

"I was scared. I thought she was going to feed me to you, as a snack."

He got the same look on his face that I got when my mother made me eat broccoli seeds. "Yuck. I hope you aren't offended, but I have no desire to eat you."

"Really? Are you sure?"

"Positive," he said with a shiver.

"Then maybe. . . ." I was afraid to say what I was thinking. He might laugh at me for even con-sidering it, but I had to try. "Then maybe we could be . . . friends?" I asked very quietly.

He looked thoughtful for a moment (it surprised me to find out I was learning to recognize a cat's expressions), and then he smiled. "You can never have too many friends."

I smiled back at him, and we sat just looking each other over for a few minutes. Then I asked him the last thing that had been bothering me. "By the way, Charlie, why didn't you tell me what a pet was the other day? It might have helped me figure this whole thing out a little faster."

He fidgeted a little. "I really didn't know how to describe it," he said. "I'm not sure exactly what a pet is, at least what people think a pet is."

"But that's easy Charlie. I figured it out right away, at least, once I started thinking about it. 'Pet' is just another word for family."

"You're right," he said with an amazed look on his face. "Wow. Are all hamsters as smart as you seem to be?"

"Only the royal ones," I said with a grin.

Chapter 18

Charlie

Oĸᴀʏ, I ᴡᴀs ᴏɴʟʏ ᴛʀʏɪɴɢ ᴛᴏ ʙᴇ ɴɪᴄᴇ when I said she was smart, but I was surprised Rose got that whole pet/family thing down so quickly. It was the perfect answer. Dad, Mom, Amanda, Andrew, Frisky, Rose and I, we are all a part of the family.

Sweet.

Rose and I talked for a while longer, and then I went to bed. It had been one long day, and I was way behind on sleep. Cats need a lot of naps, you know, and I had missed mine.

The next day was bright and sunny, a perfect spring day. I went out back to give Frisky a bad time about Rose and I having to do her job the day before, but Frisky was too excited to talk.

"He's a genius," she said as I walked out the

back door.

"Who's a genius?"

"My big, handsome love, Pepe."

Pepe? A genius? The dog that thought Frisky was a 'little lotus blossom of love'? Right. "What makes you say so?" I asked.

"He's figured out a way for us to finally see each other face to face," she said with a silly, lovesick look.

Uh-oh. I jumped up on top of the fence to figure out a way to stop this. They were both going to be crushed if they actually got a look at each other.

"Hey, Charlie, what's up man? Did you eat that ham-hock thingy yet?" Pepe called up to me.

"It's a hamster, and no, I decided to make friends with her instead." Pepe was sniffing around the bottom of the fence, like he was looking for something. "What's this I hear about you finding a way to see Frisky?"

"I been sniffing around this fence, choo know? I think maybe some of the boards are getting kinda old, and if I can find one that's weak enough, I can chew my way through into your yard, man. Then I can finally meet my sweet little love and we can have our first kiss."

There's a mental picture I never wanted.

"That's not a good idea," I said, trying to think fast and talk faster. "You see . . . um . . . it's like . . . Dad. Yeah, Dad. He . . . would get really upset if you put a hole in the fence. He would probably blame it on Frisky, and she could get punished really badly. He . . . he . . . he might even decide to get rid of her or make us move. Yeah, how would you like that? You'd feel really terrible if you got Frisky in trouble and you never got to see her again, especially right after you shared your first kiss."

He looked totally shocked. "Would he really do that, man?"

"It's very possible," I said, trying not to feel like a liar. After all, Dad might blame Frisky, and she might get punished. Dad would never make us move or get rid of her over something like that, because he loves her too much. But Pepe didn't know that.

"Rats, I thought I'd finally get to see her," he said with a sigh.

Whew, that was close.

That afternoon, as I walked by Andrew's bedroom, I saw that the door was open, so I peeked inside. Rose was rolling around Andrew's feet in her ball, and Andrew was digging everything out of his closet. I mean, everything! He had clothes, toys, books, shoes, and paper airplanes all over the floor.

I walked up to Rose. "What's he doing?" I asked.

"I don't know," Rose answered. "Looking for something I guess. I've been trying to get his attention by bumping into his feet, but he's too busy

throwing things around to notice me."

"Meow?" I said loudly.

No answer.

"MEOW!"

"Oh, hi Chawlie." Andrew looked at me with a smile. Then he looked down at Rose sitting right next to me in the ball. "You not twying to eat Wosie, are you? No, you two look like fwiends now. That's good."

"Meow?" I asked again.

"I'm lookin' for my pwetend TV. It's made of pwastic, and if I take all the insides out, I think Wose might like to pway inside it."

I looked at Rose and smiled, clearly showing that I could get answers from Andrew even if she couldn't.

"Oh great," she said. "Now all I have to learn to do is 'meow.'"

I decided to check out the closet. I'd never been able to go in there before, because Andrew always had so much stuff jammed inside that there was no room to move around. But with the contents of the closet all over the floor, I could do some exploring.

It was dark inside and kind of dusty. It reminded me of another place I had recently been, but I couldn't think of where. I made my way to the farthest back corner. There were still a few toys stacked there, all piled up behind a teddy bear that was keeping the whole thing balanced. Way back past that, I saw the purple plastic of the TV Andrew was looking for. "Meow," I said in a voice that seemed muffled by the darkness.

"What is it Chawlie? Oh, you found it!" Andrew tried to reach the TV, but the pile in front of it was too big for him to reach around. He grabbed the teddy bear to start moving the stack.

"MEOW!" I tried to warn him, but I was too late. He had already pulled the teddy, and the whole stack fell out the front of his closet with a long, loud crash.

Mom ran into the room two seconds later. She just stood there in the doorway staring at the room and taking in the toys, clothes, and random objects that were scattered all around. Then she looked at Andrew.

Andrew looked around and seemed to notice, for the first time, what he had done to his room. He looked at me, and then back up at Mom.

"Wosie did it."

In loving memory of Hilda;
a great mother, terrific mother-in-law,
wonderful grandmother,
and all around amazing woman.

Watch for Charlie's next adventure,

Charlie Goes Camping

For more information, check out
our website:

www.charliethecat.com

C.A. Goody and Charlie the cat live with their family just outside Phoenix, Arizona. Mrs. Goody wrote her first book, *Charlie's Great Adventure*, when Charlie actually disappeared and was found five days later, twenty miles from home. The book started as a short letter to her kids, as written by Charlie, explaining how he had gotten so far away. The book was such a hit with local children that Mrs. Goody continues to write stories about Charlie, who inspires ideas everyday as he finds new ways to get into trouble.

Notes to Myself

My favorite Charlie the Cat Story is:

Because:

Notes to Myself

My favorite part of this book was:

Because:

Notes to Myself

My favorite character besides Charlie is:

Because:

If I were to write a story about Charlie,
it would be called:

Because:

Notes to Myself

My favorite kind of animal is:

Because:

Notes to Myself

If I wrote a story about another animal,
it would be about:

Because: